I'm so happy when we're together.

you make me feel
ten foot tall.

You bring sunshine into my life.

All my worries disappear
when I'm with you.

I know you'll be there for me through the ups and downs.

And help me bounce back
from the bumps along the way.

To broadcast to everyone
how amazing you are.

You make
me laugh a
little louder,

Smile a little bigger ...

And live a lot more.

With you, life is double the fun.

You make me happy whatever the weather.

You are as splendid as
Little Miss Splendid.

And as cool as Mr Cool.

You make me want
to do cartwheels.

And to jump for joy.

We're never stuck for words when we're together.

There's no need to be shy
with you by my side.

Life is magic with you around.

You make the impossible possible.

And the courage
to be brave.

I know you'll always
come to my rescue.

And be there with a perfectly-fitting
hug when I need it.

But I'll just say that you are
practically perfect in every way!

This book
is for a very
special person.

LOVE

Roger Hargreaves